Fun at Camp

by Ryan Fadus   illustrated by Robin Boyer

Orlando Boston Dallas Chicago San Diego

Visit *The Learning Site!*

www.harcourtschool.com

ISBN 0-15-325478-5

4 5 6 7 8 9 10 551 10 09 08 07 06 05 04 03 02

Ordering Options
ISBN 0-15-325468-8 (Collection)
ISBN 0-15-326556-6 (package of 5)

Ned can run at camp.

Meg can hit at camp.

Rick can pass at camp.

Pam can kick at camp.

Dan can tug at camp.

Jess can bend at camp.

Look at us.
We have fun at camp!